Best Wishes,

Rick Peoples

Poetry With a Porpoise

Written by:
Rick Peoples

Illustrated by:
Susan Hart Peoples

APPENZELL PRESS
REEDERS, PA

ISBN 0-9668328-3-3

Printed in the United States of America

FOR MOM, DAD & BRIAN

Acknowledgements

Many thanks to our family and friends for their
support and encouragement. Special thanks to
John Alexander for his time and input. Very special
thanks to Tina Barisonek and George Boudman for
their contributions in putting this book together.

Also, thanks to all the educators who took the
time to offer suggestions. Your help is deeply appreciated.

An Invitation

Please color the pictures,
that you really like.
Use the colors you want,
there's no wrong or right!
One day in the future,
you can page through and look,
at how you became
a part of our book!

The Adventure

Life is an adventure,
live it to the fullest!
You're free to choose
what you think is coolest!
You can be anything,
you want to be!
Go for the top
and look what you'll see!
Find something you love
and give it your all!
Do your very best
and you'll have a ball!

1

A Good Day
(In December)

I did my homework
and studied for my test.
I was good in music class,
even tried to sing my best!
I washed the boards for teacher,
went straight home after school.
I could have tattled on my brother
but I just played it cool!
I helped Mom after dinner,
took a walk with my Grandpa!
Thank goodness it's bedtime
and I can hope that Santa saw!

Airplanes

I love to go on airplanes,
to fly to different places!
To go to other countries
and see different sights and faces.
I meet all types of people
and I never feel alone.
But the place I always
like the best, I find,
when I come home!

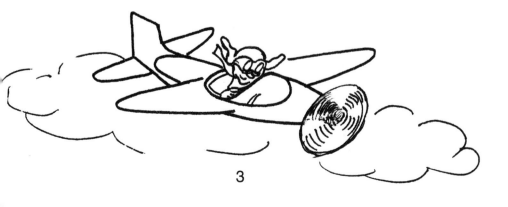

All In My Mind

I kick the field goal,
as time runs out.
It splits the uprights!
The crowd screams and shouts!

Then I make a basket,
with no time left!
My team lifts me up,
to cut down the nets!

Of course, I hit a homer
in the last of the ninth!
You see I never fail,
when it's all in my mind!

The Aquarium

We went to the aquarium.
You know, where the fishes swim.
There was all kinds of stuff to see,
things that live beneath the sea.
Creatures in all shapes and sizes,
the deep blue ocean holds surprises!

A Smile!

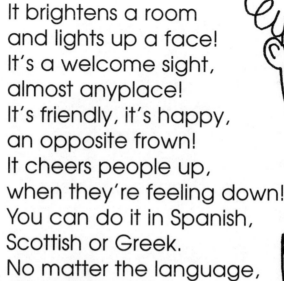

It brightens a room
and lights up a face!
It's a welcome sight,
almost anyplace!
It's friendly, it's happy,
an opposite frown!
It cheers people up,
when they're feeling down!
You can do it in Spanish,
Scottish or Greek.
No matter the language,
it's easy to speak.
You can't use it up,
'cause each one's brand new.
I know a smile, would look
good on you!

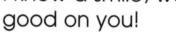

6

A Work in Progress

I know I'm not as good,
as I'd like to be.
I've got some things to
work on,
that don't come easily.
I could use a little polish,
to make me really shine!
I'm still a work in progress,
getting better all the time!

Baseball

Whizzzz ... goes the ball,
Smmmmack ... goes the bat!
Thhhump ... goes the glove,
as it makes the catch!
"Out" screams the umpire
(Why does he talk so loud?)
"Three outs for our side!"
"Yea!" cheers the crowd.

Krrunch ... goes the first pitch,
off our hero's bat!
"I got it!" the left fielder shouts,
as he starts fading back.
For a moment it's as quiet
as a whisper in the dark.
Then the place goes crazy,
as the baseball leaves the park!

Believers

The world needs believers,
you could be one!
Sometimes it's hard,
but most times it's fun!
It's a great way to live
but I should warn you,
you have to believe,
that dreams do come true!

The Blizzard

Wind fast as a cheetah,
colder than ice!
Stay by the fire!
There's a blizzard tonight!
Snow tossed from a cannon,
sideways in flight,
Like the angels in heaven
are having a snowball fight.
It could go all night
and that's all right with me!
'Cause the way that it's snowing,
there will be no school all week!

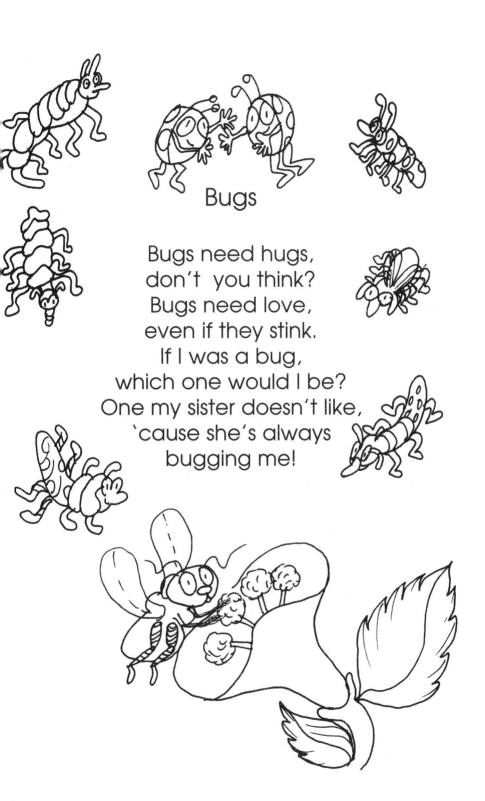

Bugs

Bugs need hugs,
don't you think?
Bugs need love,
even if they stink.
If I was a bug,
which one would I be?
One my sister doesn't like,
'cause she's always
bugging me!

Camping Out

We camped out the other night,
in a place where there were no cars.
In a forest, by a stream,
underneath the stars.
Dad showed us constellations,
they're like drawings in the sky.
Then I listened to the forest sounds,
until I closed my eyes.
When I woke up, I saw a deer
drinking from a stream.
It was hard to tell if it was real
or if it was just a dream!

The Case of the Broken Vase

I didn't mean to break it
but I did.
I meant to tell my mother
but I didn't.
I knew that was like telling
a big fib.
But I didn't think she'd
find it
but she did.

Charlie

We have a dog, named Charlie
but don't tell him, he's a dog!
I think, he thinks he's human!
(not a cricket or a frog!)
When I go to sleep at night,
he sneaks up on the bed!
I wake up each morning and
he's laying by my head!
Now by the way he's looking,
at least, I think I know.
He wants me to tell you,
that Charlie says, "Hello!"

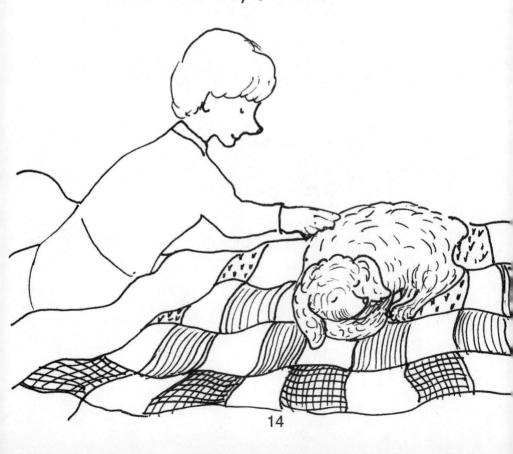

Chopsticks

We go to Chin's,
to eat Chinese
and I get to use
the chopsticks.
Though it took time,
for me to learn,
how to get the food
to my lips!
At first, it wasn't
hard to tell,
that I was a rookie.
But now I eat
just like a pro,
even, the fortune cookie!

Chopsticks, Too!

My sister taught me
a song on the piano.
I have to admit,
it's the only one I know.
The title is <u>Chopsticks</u>,
though it's hard to believe,
it has something to do
with eating Chinese.

Chores

I make my bed,
take out the trash.
I do the dishes
and cut the grass!
I work so hard,
one of these days,
I think I'll ask Dad
for a raise!

Clouds

I saw a clown up in the sky,
as I watched the clouds fly by.
He was laughing, loud and hearty,
a regular life of the party!
Then I wondered what it's like,
to put a red nose on each night
and to try to make the people laugh.
I thought this as the clown rolled past.

You wouldn't believe what came by next!
It looked like a Tyrannosaurus Rex!
A dinosaur, up in the sky
and I was a medieval knight!
We fought 'till we were soiled and tired
and like a flame that's lost its fire,
that dinosaur just disappeared,
it flew away, my victory clear!

I love to lay and watch the sky,
as fluffy clouds, go floating by.
They're anything I can imagine!
It sure beats watching television!

The Coach

He yells and screams,
he laughs, he smiles.
Enthusiasm, that's his style!
He makes us jump,
he makes us run.
We practice 'til
we move as one!
He lifts us up,
he helps us dream.
He says with pride,
that we're his team!

Dancin'!

Dancin's fun,
just move your feet
and shake your body
to the beat!
Feel the rhythm
of the song
and if you want,
sing along!

The Dark

I feel my heart beat in the dark
and my mind makes it go faster.
When it thinks of scary things,
like ghouls and ghosts and monsters.
I know there's nothing really there
but I can't convince my heart.
Because a part of me still asks
"What if?",
as I lay here in the dark.

Differences

Sometimes the people we think
we don't like,
turn out to be people we do.
Sometimes the things that we think
are lies,
somehow turn out to be true.
So don't be too quick to judge
anything,
lay back and give it a chance!
Because the difference between
notes is what makes the music
and we need it if we're going to
dance!

Don't Tell!

Don't tell anybody
but I really like school!
Don't say I said it
but I think learning's cool!
You know I'd deny it
but I love to read!
Say "thanks" to my teacher
but don't say it's from me!

End of Summer Blues

The days are getting shorter,
the summer's going to end.
Labor Day is next week
and then school will begin!
We'll have a brand new teacher
and a brand new set of rules.
I think I have a case of
the end of summer blues!

Finished?

He made the sun go
up and down.
He made the earth
go 'round and 'round.
He made the sky,
the birds, the trees,
the mountains, oceans,
you and me.
He made it all
but don't forget,
no one's said he's
finished yet.

The Fool

He thinks he's so cool!
He makes me feel like a fool,
then he goes to tease somebody else!
I'll just ignore him,
there's no need for him.
I can make a fool of myself!

Frogs

Some days I walk,
through the woods,
to the creek.
I look at the frogs
and they look at me.
They swim and
they jump,
they lay in the sun.
Frogs always seem,
like they're having fun!

Getting Bigger

This year school is harder,
than it ever was!
Though I admit we're learning,
about some awesome stuff!
There is a lot more homework
and it isn't very easy!
I sit next to this girl,
who really likes to tease me!
There's no way around it,
at least, not one that I can figure.
But life's more complicated,
now that I'm getting bigger!

Goin' Fishin'

I'm going to go fishin'!
I'm going with my Dad!
My sister's coming too
but even that's not bad!
She can catch some big ones
and she's gonna show me how!
Dad says that that's a part of,
what fishin's all about.
We're going to take the boat
and soak up lots of sun.
We'll go to that secret place
(where Dad lost the big one!)
Maybe I can catch him!
Yeah, that's my bestest wish!
But Dad says we'll have a great time
even if we don't catch fish!

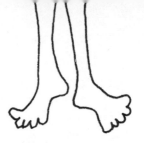

The Goldfish

Living in a glass house,
for everyone to see.
Swimming 'round in circles,
with no privacy.
A fat guy, with a giant eye,
watches as I eat.
If I were a piranha,
I think I'd start with his feet!

Growing Up

If you have to grow up,
like everyone does.
I hope you'll find something
to do that you love!
I hope you'll find something,
that makes your heart smile.
So you'll do it with love
and you'll do it with style!
You can be anything you want to be!
I hope you find something you love,
like me!

Hamsters

I don't think I'd like
to be a hamster.
Though I'm not really sure
how they feel.
I don't think I'd enjoy
spending each day,
on that stupid exercise wheel!
Spending all my life running
and not going anywhere.
I don't think I'd like being
a hamster.
But then, if I was,
would I care?

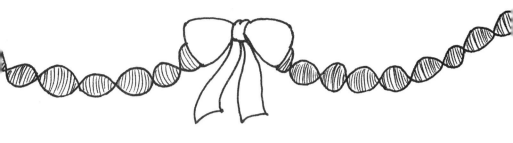

Happy Birthday
(To Me!)

It's my birthday today, so they tell me.
I don't know, I was young at the time.
I guess I was there with my mother,
after all, she'd never lie!
So somebody go for the candles!
Somebody go bake a cake!
Today is the day I was born on!
Let's party, let's celebrate!

Hiccup!

They're here and gone,
then back again.
They come and then they go!
They're uninvited guests, you see,
with a mind all of their own!
We don't know why they start with hic
or why they end with cup!
But until they decide to leave,
we do know that you're stuck!

Huh?

She does or she doesn't,
she will or she won't.
She would or she wouldn't,
she do or she don't!
She can or she can't,
she might've, could of,
maybe she'd choose me,
to be her true love!

The Hunter

The brown leaves crack beneath my feet,
though I walk carefully.
I've tracked this deer almost a mile,
though he's tried losing me.
I know I'll only get one shot,
I've got to make it count!
I must steady up my hands
and make my nerves calm down.
I hold my breath, bring up the sight
and focus with my eye.
My finger moves, the camera clicks,
the deer was sure surprised!

The Hurricane

The rain poured down,
the high winds blew,
at ninety miles per hour!
The thunder roared,
the lightning cracked
and then, our house
lost power!
We cooked dinner on
the wood stove
and played games by
candlelight.
It was a little scary
but it worked out
all right!

Interstates

Interstates are great,
when you're in a hurry.
But there's never anywhere
you can stop and pick strawberries!
You never see the little towns,
with neat lawns and church steeples.
Or stop by at the ice cream shoppe
and get to meet the people.
Yes, interstates are faster,
I really think they're fine!
But I always take the backroads,
when I have the time!

July Fourth

Swimming pools and baseball games,
family cookouts and parades!
Everybody has their ways,
to celebrate Independence Day!
It's been more than two hundred years
we've celebrated freedom here.
Fireworks light up the sky!
Hooray, it's the Fourth of July!

Kerplunk!

I love the feeling,
when I dive
into a deep
blue pool.
The way the
water rushes
by, is really
pretty cool!
I knife right
through the
water, until I
finally stop!
Then I push
off the bottom
and head back
to the top!

Life

Don't be afraid to be happy
or sad,
they're feelings of life, after all.
Don't cheat yourself of the
view from the top,
just because there's a chance
you could fall!
Deal with your fears
and they'll disappear!
Try it just once and
you'll see!
Life's a series of hurdles
you can jump over
and see just how good
you can be!

Little Bits

Life's a little bit of this
and a little bit of that.
A little bit of happy
and a little bit of sad.
A little bit of laughter
and a little bit of tears.
A little bit of bravery,
a little bit of fear.

Life is made of many things
and if it's filled with love.
Little bits of everything
else will be enough.

Making Believe

I love to pretend,
to let my mind roam.
In quiet moments,
when I'm all alone.
My imagination,
just takes me away,
to another adventure,
in some far off place.
If I'm not having fun,
then I'll just leave!
I can be where I want,
when I'm making believe.

Me, Myself and I

I was bad and was sent to my room,
just me, myself and I.
Me didn't care, myself wasn't sure
and I began to cry.
Then I went off, with myself, leaving
me alone.
It sure can get confusing,
when I'm all alone.

Mistakes

I made a big mistake today,
I do it all the time!
But today the whole class laughed
at me, even my friend, Ryan!
The teacher said that my mistakes,
won't make me a dunce!
Especially, if I make sure,
to only make them once!

He said the ones who make mistakes,
are the ones who always try!
The ones who don't, stay on the ground,
while the others learn to fly!
So I may be a pilot, of a
fighter jet someday!
And as crazy as it sounds,
mistakes may help me on my way!

47

The Moment

The moment that I wrote this,
that moment came and went.
It won't be here again, time
is like money that you've spent.
If you invest it wisely,
you'll find out that it pays.
That every moment's precious
and we should treasure
every day!

Music

It comes in through your ears
and then down to your feet.
Your toes start to tap,
fingers snap to the beat.
It comes in all styles
and each one is an art.
But music is best,
when it comes from the heart!

My Hero

The big kids made fun of me today,
they took my lunch and books away!
They teased me and they called me names,
to me, it didn't seem like a game!
Just when I was about to cry,
he came and stood right by my side.
He said he'd even up the score,
I guess that's what a big brother's for!

My Little Brother

I thought he was what I wanted.
So I waited patiently.
I taught him how to walk and talk,
so he'd play ball with me.
He must be a quick learner,
that ungrateful little brat!
Because now he beats me every time,
think I could take him back?

My Shadow

Sometimes I see it
and then it disappears!
When I'm out in the sun,
it's perfectly clear!
It's there when I get
into bed for the night.
But where does it go,
when I turn off the light?

No Charge

I love the smell of flowers,
when they bloom in the spring!
I love the sound a chorus makes,
when they begin to sing.
I love the taste of water,
from a clear, cold mountain stream.
I love a peaceful sleep,
filled with pleasant dreams.
I love my little puppy dog
and I know that he loves me.
I love the fact, that all these things,
are absolutely free!

No Limits!

When I grow up,
I might be famous.
Like that cookie guy,
you know, Famous Amos!
I just may be a movie star
or a golfer who shoots
under par!
I could be a coach,
a mechanic, a teacher,
a doctor, a soldier
or even a preacher!
There are no limits
to what I can do!
The future is waiting
for me and for you!

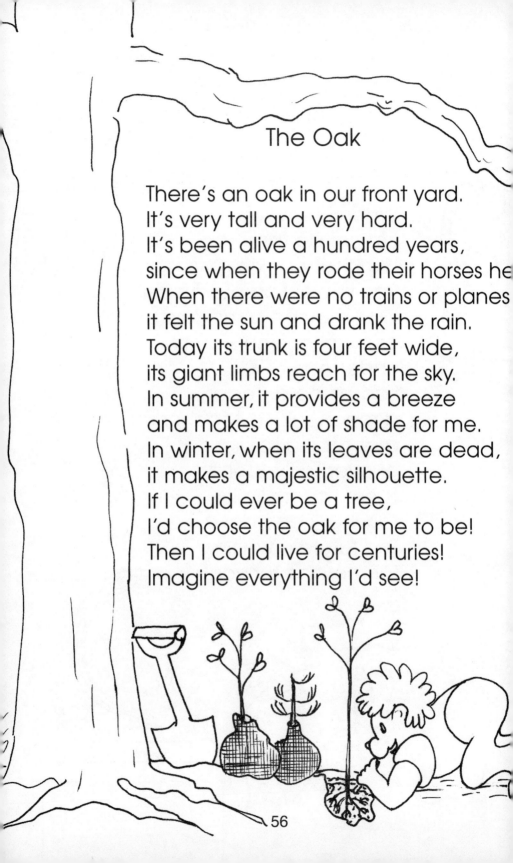

The Oak

There's an oak in our front yard.
It's very tall and very hard.
It's been alive a hundred years,
since when they rode their horses he
When there were no trains or planes
it felt the sun and drank the rain.
Today its trunk is four feet wide,
its giant limbs reach for the sky.
In summer, it provides a breeze
and makes a lot of shade for me.
In winter, when its leaves are dead,
it makes a majestic silhouette.
If I could ever be a tree,
I'd choose the oak for me to be!
Then I could live for centuries!
Imagine everything I'd see!

56

The Other Side

He says I pushed him
and he may be right.
But I wasn't the one,
who started the fight!
It's true that I pushed him
but he pushed me first!
I know I did wrong
but I think he did worse!
He'll tell you different
but this much is a fact,
one of us pushed
and the other pushed back!

Outer Space

I wonder what it's like,
to be in outer space.
To see the way the earth looks,
from another place.
To ride aboard a rocket,
to somewhere no one's been.
To stand on another planet
and then, come home again!

Overnight

My friend is staying overnight!
We're going to have a ball!
We've got videos and snacks
and an illuminated football!
We're sleeping in a tent out back,
we'll probably stay up late!
We'll tell ghost stories to scare ourselves.
I can hardly wait!

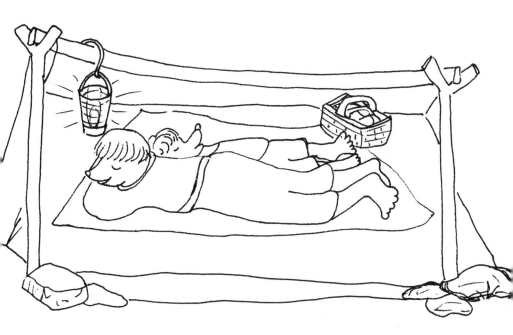

The Path

The ones who came before me,
made this path for me.
So as I walk upon it,
I must tread carefully.
And if I can make it better,
for someone else someday,
That will be my "Thank You!",
to those who helped me on my way.

Pillows

I love my pillow,
it's soft and clean.
It's shared my tears,
it's shared my dreams.
I've punched it hard!
I've held it tight
and slept peacefully,
most every night.

Problems

A lot of things start with "I can do that!",
just someone believing they can.
Then somebody else might say,
"What if?" and that is the start of a plan.
Throw in a couple of "How abouts?"
and mix in some "What if we try...?".
Then pretty soon, the problem is solved
and everyone else is surprised!

The Puddle

There's a puddle just outside our house.
Mom says to walk around it.
But that would seem like such a waste,
'cause after all, I found it!
I wonder if she'd really care,
if I put just one foot in?
Uh, oh! It's deeper than I thought!
I guess I'll go for a swim!

The Quitter

He was losing the game,
so he quit.
He didn't think he could,
so he didn't.
This was too hard
and that was unfair,
he tried very hard
to not really care.
Like a fire that just
won't stay lit,
he looked bright for
a flash,
then he quit.

The Rainout

The rain pours down,
there'll be no game.
There are puddles out by
second base.
The mounds a mess,
the outfield's wet.
The sun's somewhere,
not shining yet!
No one will win,
no one will lose.
Rainouts always
give me the blues!

Reba

Too small to be a walrus,
too big for an amoeba!
I saw a spider in the barn
and thought I'd name her Reba!
She never wrote a single word,
perhaps she just couldn't spell.
Or she didn't have a thing to say
to me, it's hard to tell.
Now it's up to me to ponder,
if she'd ever write one day.
Dad was in the barn this morning
and he had a can of Spray!

Respect

Respect has to come from inside.
It can't start from anywhere else.
Respect is like love, to give it away,
you first have to have it yourself!

Respect comes from hard work and pride,
from doing the best you can do!
When I earn and learn respect for myself,
only then. can I give it to you!

The Secret Hideout

We've got a secret hideout!
No one knows where it is!
Except for Henry, Joe and Andy,
Steve, Roger, Al and Chris!
And I told my friend, Ricky
and he told his friend, Ralph!
I guess it won't be secret long,
'cause we all have big mouths!

Some of My Favorite Things

Ice cream cones on hot days
and hot chocolate when it snows.
I like the way my feet feel,
with the sand between my toes!
Flying kites on windy days
and swimming when it's hot!
Sometimes I like camping out
and sleeping on a cot.
I like the sound the bell makes,
to announce the end of school!
There are lots of other things I like.
But these are pretty cool!

The Squirrel

There's a squirrel that lives
by my window.
I see him, most every day.
He scrunches up his nose at me
and then, he runs away.
He's rarely still, he runs and jumps,
he flies from tree to tree!
He's like a one squirrel circus act!
He's quite a sight to see!

Silence

Silence says a lot, sometimes,
if you listen hard enough.
It could be the sound you hear,
when you read a book you love.
It can underline the beauty,
of a sunrise in the fall,
mean love or hate
or good or bad,
silence can say it all!

Stress!

Don't do that!
Leave that alone!
Get out of bed!
Get off the phone!
Do your homework!
Do your chores!
Quiet down!
Don't slam the doors!
Be respectful!
Do your best!
Have you heard?
Kids have no stress!

The Strikeout

I struck out!
I let everyone down!
My teammates all moaned,
I was booed by the crowd!
I went for the fences,
that's not my style!
I swung as hard as I could
and missed by a mile!
With my third strike,
the game came to an end.
I can't wait for tomorrow,
we're playing again!

Sunrise

Through the darkest part of night time,
comes a little speck of light.
The beginning of a brand new day,
the ending of the night.
It is filled with hope and promise.
It's a slate that's fresh and clean
and we're free to write upon it,
to make it all that it can be!
Now, it won't be too much longer,
before there's a fire in the sky!
As the sun bids you good morning,
with its gift of warmth and light.

Sunset

It's going now,
painting the sky
with pinks and blues.
It's sinking now,
leaving behind its
beautiful hues.
It's almost down,
to a place that
we can't see.
It's all gone now,
just a sunset memory.

The Tantrum

Billy threw a tantrum,
he stomped his little feet!
He yelled and screamed
and flailed his arms,
it was pretty neat!
Billy through a tantrum,
he held his breath 'till he
turned red!
He cried and cried, then finally,
he did what Mama said!

Tattle-Tale

He told on me,
so I told on him!
Now, here we are,
in at recess, again!
The air's fresh outside,
in here it's stale!
I sure wish we weren't,
two tattle-tales!

Teachers

Sometimes they're funny,
sometimes they're cool.
Sometimes they make me
really like school!
They get me excited
and they make me doze.
It's amazing the questions,
whose answers they know!
They try to be fair,
everyone gets a turn.
But the best thing they do,
is they help us learn!

Teeff

My two front teeff
came out today!
The middle of my
smile's black!
It's hard to tell thum
words I thay!!
I thure hope that
they grow back!

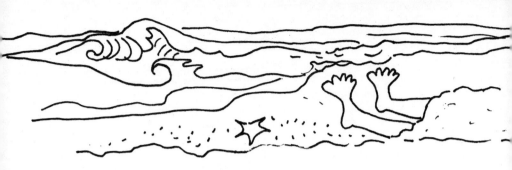

The Tide

It comes up and licks my feet,
    then scurries off again.
Do you think that it's the one,
that took my castle made of sand?
  I left it here, when I went home.
When I came back, I found it gone.
There were no footprints in the sand,
   not one sign of beast or man.
  But my castle's disappeared from sight,
do you think it might have been the tide?

Tigger

We once had a kitty,
whose paws had six toes!
They're called Hemingways
(though why, I don't know!)
We called him Tigger,
like in <u>Winnie</u> <u>the</u> <u>Pooh</u>,
because he had orange hair
and he had stripes, too!
He lived a good life,
he grew old and fat!
I'd have to say Tigger
was a mighty cool cat!

Thanksgiving

Thank you, lord for puppy dogs,
who think the world of dirty socks.
For slimy snakes and croaking frogs
and the lake where we throw skimming rocks

Thanks a lot, for summer, too!
for all the days we're off from school!
For ice cream topped with chocolate goo!
Thanks a lot, from me to you!

Today

Today's going to be a great day!
I can feel it in my bones!
Filled with friends and laughter
and hand-dipped ice cream cones!
We're going to the fun park,
gonna' try out every ride!
From the way out roller coaster,
to the too wet water slide!
There's one more thing about it,
something that's very cool!
While we are at the fun park,
my brother is still in school!

Tomatoes

Tomatoes are my favorites,
home grown, in summertime!
They're wonderful to eat just as,
you pick them from the vine!
You can slice them,
you can dice them,
you can squeeze them into juice!
Tomatoes go with everything,
in any way you choose!

The Truth

Telling the truth isn't easy
sometimes,
you have to admit you were
wrong.
And if you tell a lie, the truth
will come out
(and it usually doesn't take long!)
You can double your trouble,
by telling a lie,
or you can be honest and smart,
by telling the truth the very
first time,
before it all falls apart!

You Can Do It!

You can do it!
Yes, you can!
If you fail once,
just try again!
If you don't stop,
you'll reach the top!
The view is great
from there!

You Choose!

It doesn't matter what you do,
as long as you give it all that you've got!
You can be a plumber or a teacher
or a NASA astronaut!
You can be a painter or a pitcher
or someone who sings the blues!
Just be sure to put some pride,
in everything you do!

Weather

Whether it's cold
or whether it's hot.
Whether we like it or not.
Whether it rains
or whether it snows,
there will always be weather
you know!

Whatchamacallit

I lost my whatchamacallit,
it was with my thingamajig!
It was about so heavy,
it was about this big!
It has a doohickey on it.
Say, don't you have one
of the same?
I think that I may have
left it,
over at ol' what's his name's!

What I Don't Know

I don't know why
the big jets fly
but one day,
I will find out!
It makes me wonder,
makes me ponder,
what it's all about!
I'll look and look,
to find a book,
to tell me why it's so.
It's like a game,
I use my brain,
to find what I don't know.

What Kind?

What kind of person will you be,
one who only thinks just of themselves?
Or one who's trusted and admired
and thinks of someone else?
What kind of life will you lead,
one that's as easy as it's safe?
Or one that's filled with challenges,
to do your best each day?

What's Next?

It's right around the corner,
it waits for you, my friend.
As the clock keeps tick and tocking,
it's right around the bend!

It's always what you're going to do,
it's never what you've done!
It's always draped in mystery
and that's half of the fun!

It's exactly what will happen,
when you turn right or left.
As soon as you're done with now,
you'll find out what's next!

Who I Am

I'm the one who's in the mirror,
every time I look.
And when it comes to my life,
I'm the one who'll write the book.
It's me who's always sleeping,
right before when I wake up.
And no matter if it's bad or good,
I'm the one who'll make my luck.
In everything I'll ever do
and whatever I will be.
I'll decide just who I am,
because it's all up to me.

Winners

I had a friend,
we used to race,
he beat me every time!
I tried as hard as
I could try
but always was behind.
I huffed and puffed
and practiced
but never evened
up the score.
Though I found I could
run faster,
than I ever did before!

Uh, Oh!

I know I left him somewhere,
I fed him just today!
He was tied to something,
so he wouldn't run away.
If I could just remember,
what I tied him to,
then I could go and find him
but I don't have a clue.
So tell me if you've seen him!
Please, tell me where he went!
'Cause I'm gonna be in trouble,
if I've lost my elephant!

Your Page

The Zoo

I love to go to the zoo, don't you?
There are animals I've never seen!
They have a place, that's for the snakes
and one that's for the chimpanzees!
Some animals weigh tons
and some just weigh ounces.
They swim, they fly and slither,
one of them even pounces!
There are beautiful ones
and some that are ugly!
There are those that act shy and
those that act smugly.

Some have coats that are shiny,
some have fur that is thick.
Some have legs that are mighty
and some have legs thin as sticks!
I guess that they're like humans,
they come in all shapes and sizes.
And that's why the zoo
has so many surprises!
So the next time you're looking
for something to do,
If you can, get a friend
and go to the zoo!

The following poems are also songs. You can listen to the CD, in the back of the book and sing along with me! There are also ten readings from this book on the CD. You can find the poem and read along with me. The songs and poems are also available on cassette from:

Appenzell Press
P.O.Box 270
Reeders, Pa
18352
1-877-620-2906
www.appenzellpress.com

Dreams

Dreams come true sometimes.
It's really no surprise.
Those who try to do their best,
will be the ones to taste success.
For those who use their hearts and minds,
dreams come true sometimes.
When you reach up for the stars,
even if you fall,
you'll end up on higher ground,
standing proud and tall!
So go ahead and chase your dream
and give it all you can!
If you should fall, just get back up
and do your best again!

I Believe In You

I believe in you,
in all that you can do.
You can make your
dreams come true!
I believe in you.

I believe in me.
In all that I can be.
I hope it's plain to see.
I believe in me.

I believe in us.
In peace and hope
and love.
In a world where
people dare to trust.
I believe in us.

I Can Read!

I can read! Now the words
on the pages speak to me!
Now I can see! What it is
other people write to me.
Now I can be, anything I
really want to be.
My mom and my dad are
so proud of me.
And it's all because I can read!
I can read!
I can fly on the pages of a book!
I can find out why it rains
or how to cook.
I'll just look in a book.

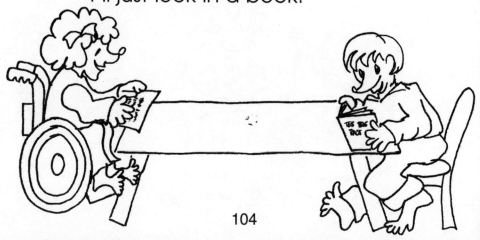

Your Song

If You Do Your Best

If you do your best, you'll
never be sorry!
If you give your all, you
just can't lose!
It won't matter what the
score is,
if you do the best that you can do!
I made the error, that lost the game,
I went home with a frown.
My eyes were leaking teardrops.
I'd let everybody down!
But dad was waiting by the door.
I guess, somehow he knew.
He told me something that day,
I'd like to share with you!

Some things will come easily
and some more difficult.
What seems simple to you,
may seem hard to someone else.
We're all good at something,
everybody has their skills.
To make the most of what you are
is one of life's great thrills!

Sam's Creek

I love to go to Sam's Creek
and listen to the frogs,
go "ribbit! ribbit! ribbit!"
as they sit upon their logs!
I watch the little minnows,
as they go swimming by
and the geese go,
"honky, honkin'", as they fly
through the sky.

Skeeters dancin' on the water,
birds are singing in the trees.
There's a magic to the stillness,
you can find down on Sam's Creek.

Sometimes I hear a beaver,
"slap, slap!" the water with its tail.
And I hear a dog "ruff, ruffin!",
the sound travels air mail!
There are fishes, snakes and lizards,
all living happily.
When you go down to Sam's Creek,
you'll never know just what you'll see!

The Silly

Can you clap your hands fast?
Can you stomp your feet slow?
Can you roll your eyes around,
move your head to and fro?
Can you do it all at once?
You know I thought you could!
It looks a little silly
but it sure feels good!

Can you quack just like a duck?
Can you waddle all around?
Can you flap your little wings?
It's a silly sight and sound!
Can you do it all at once?
You know I thought you could!
It looks a little silly
but it sure feels good!

110

Why Not Me?

Someone's going to be the best,
someone's going to live their dream.
Someone's going to win the game,
someone will, why not me?

Someone's going to find the answers,
someone will make history.
Someone's going to fly that rocket,
someone will, why not me?

Because tomorrow has no limits,
the future holds no boundaries.
Someone's going to change the world,
someone will, why not me?

Someone's going to write the next song,
someone will make the next movie.
Someone's going to be a leader,
someone will, why not me?

Someone's going to cure a patient,
someone will teach a child to read.
Someone's going to make a difference,
someone will, why not me?

The Wish

If you had one wish,
that would come true,
what would you wish?
What would you do?
Would you wish for fame?
Would you wish for wealth?
Would you go for power
or for good health?
Would you cure the sick?
How about world peace?
If you had one wish,
what would that wish be?

If I gave a day to you,
where would you go?
What would you do?
Would you stay home?
Would you take a flight?
Climb a mountain?
Ride a bike?
Would you have some fun,
would you sing the blues?
If you had one day,
what would you do?

If you had one life
and you could do,
anything with it,
you wanted to.
Would you do well,
give it your best?
Would you work hard
and find success?
Or spend your life
just being cool?
If you had one life,
what would you do?

Well, friends I've got
news for you!
You've got one life,
what will you do?